Red Owl

By the same author

Zirconia Poems

Red Owl

Poems by Robert Morgan

W · W · NORTON & COMPANY · INC ·

NEW YORK

Copyright © 1972 by Robert Morgan
FIRST EDITION
ALL RIGHTS RESERVED
Published simultaneously in Canada
by George J. McLeod Limited, Toronto

Library of Congress Cataloging in Publication Data

Morgan, Robert.
   Red owl; poems.

   I. Title.
PS3563.087147R4   811'.5'4   72–5473
   ISBN 0–393–04293–6
   ISBN 0–393–04136–0 (pbk.)

PRINTED IN THE UNITED STATES OF AMERICA

1 2 3 4 5 6 7 8 9 0

for Nancy

Contents

I

II

III

x

Acknowledgments

I wish to thank the following publications for first printing these poems:

Lillabulero: "Topsoil," "Whippoorwill," "The Drained Lake," "Planting," "Finding an Old Newspaper," "Ghost Tracks," "Great-grandmother," "Copper," "Church Pews," "Time," "Seismograph," "Weed Above Snow," "April 1970," "Bees Awater," "Wind," "Warm Winter Day," "Stove," "Building a Dam," and "Woodpile"
Mill Mountain Review: "Earthquake," "Spring," "Cedar," and "Hubcabs"
The Brown Bag: "White Pines," "Mendicant Rose," and "Cold"
The Greensboro Review: "Toolshed," "Meteor," and "Bonfire"
The Nation: "Chestnut," "Windfall," and "Present"
Dragonfly: "Cellar" and "Slide"
Fly by Night: "Old Photograph" and "Light Is Bleached"
Sumac: "Exhaustion" and "2 A.M."
The Allegheny Star Route: "Hog-wire Fence"
The Carolina Quarterly: "He Hoes Forever"
30/6: "New-plowed Ground"
The Southern Poetry Review: "Day Lilies"
The Stone: "Red Owl"
New American Review: "House Burning"

Several of the poems in this book were first printed as a pamphlet by the Angelfish Press. Special thanks to David Sykes.

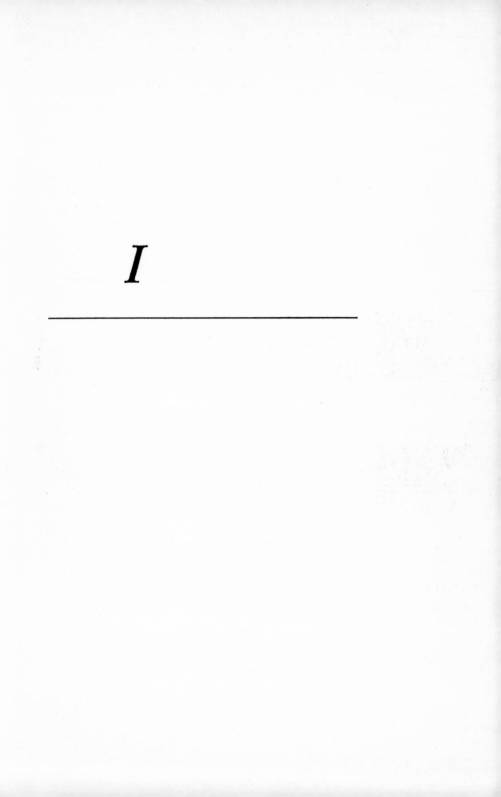

I

I

Topsoil

Sun's heat collects in leaf crystals
crumbling.
Earth grinds the grain
to dark flour, drifts black flannel
over rock and clay.
Life invests
and draws on.
A lake rises over the world,
heaps of the rotting ocean.
Sun's heat adding
weight
piles on its light
century after century tarnishing
earth's metal.
Traffic of roots
hurrying. Places the raw meat
shows through torn to the quick.
Red clay mirrors.
Black fruit
growing around the earth, deepening
in the autumn
sun drifting down.

Cellar

The air moves as if something just left.
Snake breath.
Cool razors circulate
touching the skin with wet silk.
Breathing clear cheese.
Mold flowers grow like plastered snowballs
on the walls, rust-lacquered pipes.
The heads of translucent shoots crawl out of the potato bin
and run like wires to the window.
Once cut straight and firm
the walls have dripped and rotted to black jelly.
Jam grows blue fur.
The light bulb flickers as if circled by moths
fanning its coolness
and lighting on my neck.
Walls sweating mercury, straining
to the weight. . . .

Woodpile

Chips surround the block
like foam
around a fountain
or bread scattered for the earth's fish,
packed in strata
for each winter survived
before rotting,
maple oak and apple,
fibers intertwining as they soak
into the ground, echoes
from each blow of the ax.

Well

A deep hoofmark left when the buildings are gone.
When you push away the vines
and look into the tower
an eye at the top watches you back.
Birds fly away
from the rock dropped in.
Here men and women drank from the earth
through a reed that held them by a tether
of thirst.
The well was a root they sunk
to maintain their hold here, a mineshaft
strong as the battlement of a buried city
for tapping the secret passages.
As you look the reflecting lens
imposes your silhouette on the stars.
This tree with its leaves of men
died from the top down.

Building a Dam

Two ways to make a pond.
Shovel a hole in the gravel under the stream
and let it fill (as it eventually will with silt)
or shovel up just enough mud
and rock to trap
the branch at a narrows,
to catch up a deep area of water
stretching around the bend,
up coves and tributary branches,
rising over weeds and cowtrails.
But after the dam is built, after you
throw a body of mud and clay
on the skeleton of brush
and tamp, covering
with turf,
and while the cold water
is rising every minute, extending
further back on itself and its feeders,
hushing the saults and covering muskrat slides,
there is the problem of a spillway.
Because no matter
how long delayed the stream
will reassert its motion and slice
a groove in the waterlogged turf and clay
or brush the whole project out of its way the first rain.

Windfall

Falling away from itself the oak
raises a helm of roots
steering it
back into the earth.

Bass

In the graveyard at the upper end of the lake
trees lie out from their stumps like shadows,
a log jam rising in late summer
bleached and knot-eyed.
Moss wigs.
Stumps clear the water
on roots. Blue gills flip
like coins at the surface. Minnows
sprinkling.
A tent of algae
is draped. In its shade
a hollow log is watching.

Rubies

Washed out where the stream unbraids
over mud and gravel (water selects
sand and leaves
the heavier fragments)
rubies wait
for a freshet to carry
them on. Each hard rain they descend
the valley a little and are buried
again, sometimes overgrown.
Weeds thrive,
their roots enclosing
insights, pieces broken
from the lurid brain inside
the mountain,
the beacon behind
the springs and up crevices,
bloodshot, aiming darkness. Aims
the terrible centuries
of heat and weight
into its perfect
structure,
its burning shattered
and worked out by the mountain's
lurching, scattered downvalley in separate
embers under moss, in mud.

Reach

Where the rockledge broke away
the huckleberry bush
has run its roots
out through a fissure
to the crevice and down several
yards past a hornet's nest
to another ledge
where slate chips have piled
like rotting leaves, and lichens and moss
have caught an inch or two of dirt.
Other roots have run back into the cliff
tapping the drip from rain
caught inside the mountaintop.
Thin roots have explored
all cracks
and grown like wedges
and slow charges of dynamite
prying off and disfiguring the cliff,
leaving their infiltration
exposed,
the support and supply
of the bush in jeopardy.
But succeeding in the long
drawn-out destruction to new land.

Resin

The pine is smeared with salves,
has thick scabs
and dripping sores.
The spinal fluid runs out
thickening a pouch around itself.
Reddish milk festers
from knotholes
hardening to quartz.
Boiled its spirits return
as oil, an intelligence,
colorless, volatile,
vehicle of color and solvent.
A whiff burns.
But the pine's sweet
blisters balm the air.

White Pines

Standing beneath huge pilings.
Up there where the sea broke, browsed along the sand
millions of years ago.
A faint surf breaks far overhead.

Wagon Roads

The wagon road was made by plowing around
the mountain with a moldboard
after the rocks had been pried out
and the main roots cut.
A furrow was plowed several times deep
and then leveled by dragpans
and shovels.
Rocks were tamped
into the branchbeds for a footing
under water and to prevent further erosion.
Rockslides and windfalls caused
the worst damage,
and thaw deflating the surface.
Low-hanging laurels had to be watched out for
and rattlers sunning on the rocks above.
The spring by the road had a can
on a stick.
The roads ran up high
to avoid marshes. But cars didn't follow
and they were left for logging and hunters,
drifting full of leaves.
When the trees are bare they wander
like trails etched by worms, unsure, getting lost
in coves, but always converging at gaps.

Muddy Road

Etching into permafrost
wheels slice through the suction of a hundred mouths
kneading and tearing off
as spokes tie knots
in the thick-lipped ruts.
The clay is so jagged it blisters
vision, like honey under a microscope.
Heaps of random carvings and blottings. Wakes
fill and wash smooth.
The road quivers as a body
when jarred.
Now the earth itself is a lubricant,
squirms and squints bubbles
as a hoof sinks in
and pops out like a cork,
and the crater fills with old blood.
Treads are written over each other
and over yesterday's palimpsest of fossils.
Turds of subsoil are squeezed up.
Springs seep through
filling each track with warped sky.
Night, the road's history is set in stone.
Slashed grooves, puddles stranded.

Wire Grass

A star explosion, and the streamers, debris,
set off new stages where they touch
and are nailed down by roots.
To leap off again
skipping over ground.
Each new base fires out filaments
that overlap and dive under
the parent systems,
weaving a wire mat over
dirt, a web trapping sunlight
and area, not halting at water
but throwing its tendrils
across, floating
them out until they catch
or get washed back by the current.

Mound Builders

To place a bump on the land, something
to rub the horizon, to climb
around and sit on
looking out over lakes and trees
level with the sun.
A place to walk spelunking
close to the black dirt where stars grow.
The mound rises to warn
intruders
and to last,
strewn with the bones of eaten animals
and oyster shells, and our bones.
The dirt is our ancestors.

Speaking

To roll rocks off mountains
you set them up like monuments and push.
They start out slow,
staggering, out of alignment,
but generate stability,
blurring over logs,
crashing, bobbing
up again like deer till out of sight.
And still you hear them running away all the way
to the bottom and stop, coinlike, in the leaves.

Thaw

Rods and cones
at the ends of fingers held up to the sun.
Snakes work in their roots of sleep
and dirt shows through
a huge fingerprint in the field.
Hiss of crystals breaking
as sun renders out the fat in snow
to run and be drawn to the sky again.

Slide

High on the mountain's gable
a raft of dirt loosened by the wet spell
tears away and spills
over
flattening the trees below
and bulldozing roots and boulders,
opens springs
in the mountain and spreads to the pasture.
Dirt squeezed high in the air
and packed for millions
of years crawls out
and pours.
For the mountain is burning down,
its tallow oozes to rest.

The Drained Lake

I walk into the fields like Noah
stepping again on dry land.
A fish swims off into the weeds for the first time.
The hills are draped in folds of mud.
I walk through damp valleys
crossing the ocean floor.
A stump is covered with old bass plugs
and carp rot in puddles.
Below the muddy fields and meadows
of stumps, a clear stream is running.

Land has risen from the sea again.
I follow the receding water,
climb wet dunes
looking for a place to build a city in the dark silt.
Already ferns of erosion grow into the hills
following springs to their source,
mining heaps and deposits
of topsoil and carrying them away,
black grease of rotten leaves.
Already the uplands are cracked and curling,
strewn with broken pottery; the paint
peels from old boards,
revealing sand.

We turn toward the desert,
cut down the trees and walk over them
exposing the secret places, drain sloughs

and open springs to the drying wind.
This is the quest for extinction, translating
motion into landscape,
walking the clean bridge of sand
that falls through an hourglass building
a tiny mound of salt.

New-plowed Ground

Plow enters under dead weeds,
opens a seam to the creek.
With wings I could plow the sea.

> Curving black surf across the hill,
> blade shine on clods,
> foam of roots and stubble.
> You can't navigate without
> getting dirt in your shoes. Squeak
> of plowed-up field mice.

> Walk the rut it's easier,
> ground carved off a foot down.

Smell of water underground, cellars opened,
wormwet, cunt soft,
> washing toward rye.

Planting

Powder the furrow with salt
mined from the air. Wading the dirt. Crushing soft clods
like strawberries.

> Corn—four to the hill
> Beans—one, white submarines traveling
> underground, lifting into the sun,
> birth of leaves from a bivalve.

Mining the hill with seeds,
green fountains splash in my tracks.
The earth a dark swamp, old hen settin
on seeds.

Sun leaves the dirt a brick
icecap.
> Briarshoals dying.

He Hoes Forever

Heat is a vacuum around the body filling with sweat.

Clods on the warped hill, chunks
of red brick and dying potato vines.
The fence wanders, rusty vine curling through weeds.
The pasture has filled to a lake of briars,
wave on wave of flowers rowing
where once the white horse ran.

He hoes the rocks, the afternoon, he hoes forever.
Cornpatch swung on the hill like a cape,
fields draped from the horizon,
clod tapestries.

The mountains wet blue tents watching.

Hog-wire Fence

Rust mortar still
holds a few bricks of air,
but the net seining others from
property and holding it in from the continuing
terrain is ruptured
and hard to find among the weeds
as a century-old deed in the courthouse.
Disappears turning over like a Möbius strip.
Runs through the middle of trees.
Otherwise the fence holds up
its rotting posts.
The tennis of ownership is played elsewhere.

Boredom

When the creek shifts intentions
and whips the other shore
scooping
a new pool with the weight
of its turn,
the backwater spins
to a stop and fills.
Silt falls out gentle as light snow
and the water clears itself
with no hope of moving on.
Sun sweetens the water with algae,
ropes of frog eggs.
The surface is plucked
by mosquitoes.
Land rises inside
and weeds grow out
to the new channel.
While the creek saws away saws away
only leaving.

Birling

The tree falls like a spoke turning into the hill,
drops and does a pushup
kicking back off the stump.
The chainsaw eats meat, bawls like a calf,
its tongue licking sunlight.
Dust rears a feather.
Held the ax
so long it hurts to let go.
Snaking logs down the groove.
They revolve in the pond nudging
and making room.
A wailing starts in the sawmill.

Ghost Tracks

Rolling up the carpet of snow in the yard
to make a snowman
we collect embossed chicken tracks
and tire treads made over
a month ago
by a rooster we killed for Christmas
and a tread already worn off, scattered like ashes
over the roads and smeared on pavements.
What we have is an almost perfect
replica while it lasts,
and as a great-aunt dying in January
said to her husband,
"You'll be married again before
my tracks are gone from the yard."
And he was.

Earthquake

A ghost dance of trees bowing,
breaking.
Pianos are launched like speedboats.
Hear the gods walking,
their tracks resonate like drums,
spreading in circles, dribbling basketballs in lockers.
Lovers lying face to face have the best
position for survival.
Gravity circles like wolves,
biting its tail.
One second the ground heaves
like a forest
then falls away to cliffs
at the world's edge.
There is no sacrifice to offer.
There is no sacrifice to offer.

Whippoorwill

The dead call at sundown from their places
on the mountain and down by the old mill.
They rise from the cellars of trees
and move up and down the valley
all night grazing like deer.
The call:
a rusty windmill creaks on the prairie.
Bats dipping and rising on ski jumps
are antennae
receiving and transmitting the code.
The whippoorwill interprets the news
from the dead, the unborn.

Exhaustion

The earth is our only bed, the deep
couch from which we cannot fall. Suddenly
this need to lie down.
The flesh will flow out in currents of decay,
a ditch where the weeds find dark treasure.

II

II

Present

Our alchemy must be secret.
On cold moss
the redhot salamander.
Now is the dictionary of everything.
Doorway.
A place to stand.

Toolshed

The sticky smell of rust breaking out in blisters
after every wet spell and burning hoeblades, plows,
crowds the eaves with dryness and wets the lower air.
Dust is stuck to the greased singletree.
Wasp nests like gray sunflowers
hang from tin. The air here hasn't moved
in thirty years, old snow hovering above ground.
Pale weeds grow to cracks.
Half-eaten shovels lean on plows
caked with forty-year-old mud.
Dust drifts crossed by snake zags. Broken clevis.
Plow points are nailed like rusting leaves
to the rafters. Dauber combs dripping plaster.
A bird looks out of its nest in the corner like a dragon
lurking. 1936 license plate,
hames sucked weightless by dry rot.

House Burning

Came to see the house shine like quartz dilating
and spinning its facets in the sun,
so bright you can tell exactly where the flame
ends and the clear air begins.
Wood transfigures, a place leaving.
The fire gives X-ray vision
through the rooms
where boards sweat resin
and ribs and soaring rafters are wrapped
tightly in flames.
Came to see the bird catch fire
and fall into the basement where cartridges
go off in a close private war.
Hot air rushes out a hundred yards over
the faces of onlookers who came as to a hanging to see
the family sitting on a rescued sofa under
the apple trees watching
the fire preach its sermon over the pyre.
Ash circles like buzzards
in the smoke rising straight up before it scatters,
huge pencil scrawling on the sky.

Came to see the black cage of studs and rafters falling
in, the timbers of black feathers,
black satin crumbling

in sour clay to nurse unheard
of growth of crabgrass.
The old folks living in a trailer around the hill,
the kids in ranch houses nearby.
Two chimneys facing above the cornfield.

Cedar

Smell the recorders buried here.
Music lies in the wood
as in the cat's entrails, in ore.
Faint musk of old arrows, canoe ribs.
Wood still giving
its breath, radioactive—releasing
a subtle verb for years
to fill whatever room or closet it lies in
till it's dark, inert
as the wood of cathedral carvings.
Weather leaches the glow
and withes of cool air plunder the fibers. The heat
is drunk off.
The wood reveals in lessening quanta the spice
from a country no one has seen,
leaking from a broken limb expanding to nonexistence.
But inside the scent's strong as light; it repels
the moth as two ends of a magnet
shun meeting.
For they are from the same country, the smell
lunar, musty, an ember so cool
you can hold it in your hand, and the moth
burning out of the dark, its semiquaver
weak as a photograph emerging in the darkroom pan.

Great-grandmother

Her skin like the gray paper of a hornet's nest
is frightening to touch.
As though you might receive a shock
this close to the strange meat of death.

Chestnut

Opening a chestnut we find a huge eye
staring between whiskered lids.
This animal gone to extinction left
its eye to remind us
we're being watched
through the earth's dark lens.

Finding an Old Newspaper
in the Woods

The sheets are exposed like film
photographing the gray and yellow seasons of decay.
The weather has flattened them to coarse
paper of leaves and pine needles.
They are almost dust.
The print has crawled off
and gone back to live with the ants.

Mendicant Rose

Alive on this tree of blood.
The bear snoring
in the heart breathes out
to the frontiers and pulls in again
as the ocean sends its roots
to the highest springs,
retrieving its gift.
A warm rain of blood falls on the slopes
and turns homeward,
spending its money all the way.
O mendicant rose.

Old Photograph

The glow from this tiny window, the distance
stuck to paper. The sunlight of seventy years ago selects
each wrinkle and thread of his coat, each whisker,
swells in the viscosity of her glasses.
Her breasts weigh on the brooch-gathered dress
like tallow pulling from a candle.
The house juts, each separate splinter of grass
aimed, carved in the old light.
Unpainted boards flare away from nails.
His bootstrap flops.
Sharp trees blowing.
They stare beyond as your eye
takes them again.
They stand at a threshold looking far behind you.

Copper

The meat of the sun is still pink inside.
But the skin's deceptive,
growing mossy barnacles
on bullets.
Drinks electricity.

Squeeze the juice out.
The lights are still on inside.
Molecules beating like pistons.
Hypnotic presence.
All metal is evil.

Stove

The fire whines its distant
siren and the stove door grins like a jack-o'-lantern
chewing its mouthful of flames.
The family gathers
like petals around the hot
black stem, bees returning.
Once a week the stove is cooled and polished
like leather, the flightdeck top
disassembled revealing
the depths the coals inhabit.
The stove is an extra digestive tract,
a vehicle for translating
the ancient vegetable
heat to the present.
Inside the fire runs its circuitry
and subroutines making split-second chemical
decisions.
The stove is motor.
Tobacco juice ferments in the bucket of ashes.
Later the heat returns and vanishes
through the coals.
The campfire dies while the hunters
are off hunting.
A sour wet silence pours down the stairwell.

Faucet

Water arrives from below
gargling in the long steel taproot.
Trickles gather
on the spigot's rim
and stretch away tangling.
A thin globe is blown
from the threaded lips
leaking
its knowledge
in tatters that form
perfect drops before hitting.
Bores out a solid auger.
Behaves
and misbehaves
surprising itself.
Water arrives blinking in the sun,
crawls away on the grass.

Bubble

The drop inflates like the spit
a glassblower speaks into, or you breathe
against the window till the pane
stretches out in a fluttering
sock and breaks off
healing
instantly to a perfect sphere.
Drifts wobbling out past the juniper.
Rainbows coil on the surface.
Wind distorts
the pneumatic toughness.
Encloses an embryo of space
beyond reach.
Glides spinning
into the grass and vanishes
to mist.

Church Pews

Under dust's upholstery
the wood itself still has the polish
of an apple,
the work of generations
of twisting children.
Salt is still in the grain
from afternoon singings and revivals.
The oil from sweating hands
and the rubbing of sweaty cloth
have left a finish
that sparkles
long after paint has cracked
and peeled, and in spite of the names carved
and figures drawn with pocketknives.
Only nailheads have rusted through the shine.
The pews are arranged like coffins
in a mausoleum.
It's like visiting an old courtroom
where you touch the wood expecting it to vibrate
with the voices of accuser and condemned.
The abandoned theater
will not perform.

Time

Snow-covered peaks gather in the north
like arabs talking.
You can't be sure you see them
but they leave an afterimage, detached
from the horizon, floating on haze.
Ragged seconds around the sky's dial.
If you look long enough they seem to march
like bishops shuffling toward hell.
I know the ground is a bridge
leading there—
to the white tents
and altitudes of death—
but I don't believe it. I don't
believe you can get there by just walking
the earth one step after another,
but must be snatched miraculously away,
fall upward into the terrible
blue emptiness.
When I stand in a field
the field and I are a sundial.
But the body alone is a clock, and each
motion it makes.
Something must distract us, anything.
The cornfield slapping in the rhythm of a tennis game,
a crow flying his clockhands on a face
without surface.
The will always hungry.

Seismograph

Its hand goes on writing a letter
without stopping,
describes the ocean
throwing up shovels of water
like a gravedigger who never rests.
Hard to imagine
since we can only hold something
in mind by finding a corner or crack,
somewhere it stops and isn't.
Like thinking about death.

The ear's tiny seismograph is always writing,
but to understand
we must break up the account
into segments,
to hear the music.

Weed Above Snow

Folded like the meat of a walnut in sleep the worm
in his high minaret, the bulb on the weed stalk rocked by wind,
dreams of you thinking of him.
This poem the space between two mirrors.

Stump

You come upon a full basin, a level pool
of wood in which circles spread
imperceptibly
from the tiny seedling trapped inside.
Now that it's over we read a topographic map
of the tree's lifetime,
the concentric measures uneven,
stretched out
of shape by root dispersal,
only approximating the pattern
but succeeding
each other, counting
the years until the history breaks off.

III

Red Owl

The sun is awake all night
flying unseen
through the earth searching
streams and caverns for prey, counting
the buried metals and feeding on blackness,
moist stenches, vapors of sleep.

She goes down herding light through crevices and roots,
through mud and the leaflike veins
where milk grows in the sleeping cows.

Rivers pour east to float her into view
and shadows lie down
for her rising, then travel across
to the next valley
on pilgrimage
to the ranges beyond her.

They are the eye's dream behind the light.

April 1970

"Buds crack like hatching eggs."

Each bears the sun's lush image
like a thumbprint.
I touch this leaf, this map
for the blind.

Bees Awater

You find one drinking at the creek,
scratching and drinking
before take-off.
He lifts back
and takes aim, firing homeward.
That's the moment to get your sighting,
get the direction and slant of climb
and you'll be looking right at the tree
on the ridge above
where the honey hangs inside
like cells of a battery
charged with sweetness.
The whole tree has the hum of a transformer.
Bees bubble, circling
like electrons.

Though excited as before a holdup
and hot from the long climb,
you drop the ax
and wait for dark.

2 A.M.

A dog barks through the horn of a valley.
Low moon burning in a cedar.
The creek mutters like an old woman
who walks in her sleep among the trees
dreaming of the life after death
when she will lie down like the stream
and flow to the darkness.

Meteor

A spike is driven in the air
so hard sparks fly.
I look up in time to see the meteor
losing its feathers
through the hourglass night,
as a hawk seizing its own death,
murderous for self-extinction.

Aspire

The breath of water leaves its body
frantic with ambition
toward the sun,
only to be frozen in the rare
altitudes and abandoned by the light,
to gather and begin the long fall
back to itself,
to the slavery of carrying
the earth's debris.
Yet sure as Avogadro's number
it rises, purified by the journey.

Power

The stream trots like an immortal dog on the wheel,
varies its pace only with flood and drought,
searching for the earth's center.
Not even stopping at walls
but climbing on its own shoulders over.
For the sun lifts up a great counterweight
of ocean that falls
pressing everything to motion,
stretching twigs on the forests of mines.
And the earth reverses the weights automatically.

Even the little spring here is compelled,
raises its head striking,
pulls on its roots,
cannot lie still.

Wind

Spirits revive, return from their journeys.
You step into the thrust of music,
lean into a great voice, the long muscular syllable.
We are thirsty for the wind
carrying its mirage, the great door closing
and closing far off with a sonic boom.
The air is off balance,
falling over and over itself like an avalanche
of leaves. Lightning rides the ridge
hurling its lasso.
The long shout drives it to its nests.
A cave unfurls like a parachute behind me,
follows, a clear shadow
pushing like a candle as the darkness
inside tries to soak through.

Warm Winter Day

Pines rise like shadows aimed north of the sun,
rivers shining down oaks.
I relax to the ground looking
into space (the great blue seed) like an exile
turning homeward.
An acorn lies near my eye, long brown breast.
The sun is a spring feeding
the wide blue valley.
Whiskers and spokes of fire twist across the distance
like a rope bridge in Asia.
The black hole behind the sun
hurls its dungeons.
You must go into the wilderness alone.

Day Lilies

The sudden appearance on roadbanks and along
ditches, in weeds where nothing has been seen.
Each stretching to get a look,
returned
the color of a salmon
to the spot its parent marked for a day,
risen from the dark by searching
root deltas,
the red climbing headwaters
to burst the stem's thermometer.
By trails and isolated meadows, speckled
in the updrafts,
each jumping
clitoris of color.
Meditating like Tibetan monks,
tracking the sun.
Tonight they roll up like cigars.
As wind blows they rock
the earth, make it pitch and run.

The Spring

Kneel and look into the quiet
hermetic valley, desert of broken armor,
sand beacons.
The breath of underground islands lifts to the sun.
Horizon feeds
on the dark hill of space
where the dead go.
Smoke of extinct tribes in quartz.

Light Is Bleached

Light is bleached by dust and insects
torture space, creak like rusty springs in the grass
where the sprinkler swings
a rope of water on the lawn
and last greens echo drowning under
yellow, and mud is sharpened by the sun.

The arches of the mole are cracked by drought.
Drugged by cold insects gather to the warmth of boulders,
pokeweed dripping berries.
The lake aims a totem of reflections at the red maple.
Squeezed like beads of oil from the hard ground
ants march south.

Dirt piled by ditches is still warm, heavy tents
settling as the sun draws through pines
dripping strings of honey.

Flocks of yellow fly from the poplar.

Rabbit Tobacco

Seeking magic, the journey,
children collect and hoard the earlike leaves
for smoking in attics and cedar groves,
lighting the fuse of adolescence.
Fire's rapid decay exhilarates,
lungs eat vegetation's death.
The spark swells
like a track in melting snow
to cover the leaf,
and the ashes are scattered carefully.

Bonfire

I say the book flutters its pages like a nugget
(fountain peeling itself)
of excited air
remembering the magma.

Milk Gap

Climbing up into the gap between day and evening,
to the saddle of trampled dirt,
to meet the stock
halfway coming down
from the ridges and balds.
Their tinkling closes in from hollows
and rides downdrafts.
Hogs burst
from the undergrowth
heavy with roots and acorns,
come for a few scraps.
The young bull dominates to the shuck rack.
Cows hook to get a position, banging
the brass flowers on their necks.
Their calves feed from behind.
Sun takes aim
through here.
Throw down the stool
and milk quickly. The cow turns
to watch her strange calf.
The voice of the bucket
hushes as it fills.

Cold

Chicken droppings chalk the yard and boot tracks
are soled with ice.
Bright as the light in a rose clouds lean, converging on the west.
Hay and sorghum breath of cattle eating
warms the loft where wind cuts like rays through cracks.
Snow on the northern slopes losing its voice as the sun goes down.
The yard is a floe of wind which I must swim going home,
ruts freezing leathery, then stone.

Hubcaps

The tractor runs over dirt and shapes it, turning
stubble and moving the hill
furrow by furrow to the terraces,
slicing clods, wearing
them away and chopping roots
to rot in sweet beds of decay.

The owl: eyes like arenas
gathering
the weeds and hungry ditches.
She guards the air like a monument
shedding a field of energy downwind.

Old hubcaps burning all night in the creek.